THIS BOOK BELONGS TO

_____

THE ADVENTURES OF

REDDY FOX

THE ADVENTURES OF

REDDY FOX

THORNTON W. BURGESS

*With Interior
Illustrations by*
HARRISON CADY

SEA
GRASS

TABLE OF CONTENTS

There was Farmer Brown's boy,
sure enough.

GRANNY FOX GIVES
REDDY A SCARE

R EDDY FOX lived with Granny Fox. You see,
Reddy was one of a large family, so large that
Mother Fox had hard work to feed so many hungry
little mouths and so she had let Reddy go to live
with old Granny Fox. Granny Fox was the wisest,
slyest, smartest fox in all the country round, and
now that Reddy had grown so big, she thought it
about time that he began to learn the things that
every fox should know. So every day she took him
hunting with her and taught him all the things that

she had learned about hunting: about how to steal Farmer Brown's chickens without awakening Bowser the Hound, and all about the thousand and one ways of fooling a dog which she had learned.

This morning Granny Fox had taken Reddy across the Green Meadows, up through the Green Forest, and over to the railroad track. Reddy had never been there before and he didn't know just what to make of it. Granny trotted ahead until they came to a long bridge. Then she stopped.

"Come here, Reddy, and look down," she commanded.

Reddy did as he was told, but a glance down made him giddy, so giddy that he nearly fell. Granny Fox grinned.

"Come across," said she, and ran lightly across to the other side.

But Reddy Fox was afraid. Yes, Sir, he was afraid to take one step on the long bridge. He was afraid that he would fall through into the water or onto

the cruel rocks below. Granny Fox ran back to where Reddy sat.

"For shame, Reddy Fox!" said she. "What are you afraid of? Just don't look down and you will be safe enough. Now come along over with me."

But Reddy Fox hung back and begged to go home and whimpered. Suddenly Granny Fox sprang to her feet, as if in great fright. "Bowser the Hound! Come, Reddy, come!" she cried, and started across the bridge as fast as she could go.

Reddy didn't stop to look or to think. His one idea was to get away from Bowser the Hound. "Wait, Granny! Wait!" he cried, and started after her as fast as he could run. He was in the middle of the bridge before he remembered it at all. When he was at last safely across, it was to find old Granny Fox sitting down laughing at him. Then for the first time Reddy looked behind him to see where Bowser the Hound might be. He was nowhere to be seen. Could he have fallen off the bridge?

"Where is Bowser the Hound?" cried Reddy.

"Home in Farmer Brown's dooryard," replied Granny Fox dryly.

Reddy stared at her for a minute. Then he began to understand that Granny Fox had simply scared him into running across the bridge. Reddy felt very cheap, very cheap indeed.

"Now we'll run back again," said Granny Fox.

And this time Reddy did.

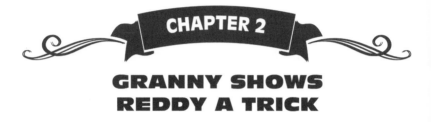

CHAPTER 2

GRANNY SHOWS
REDDY A TRICK

EVERY DAY Granny Fox led Reddy Fox over to
the long railroad bridge and made him run
back and forth across it until he had no fear of it
whatever. At first it had made him dizzy, but now
he could run across at the top of his speed and not
mind it in the least.

"I don't see what good it does to be able to run
across a bridge; anyone can do that!" exclaimed
Reddy one day.

Granny Fox smiled. "Do you remember the first
time you tried to do it?" she asked.

Reddy hung his head. Of course he remembered—remembered that Granny had had to scare him into crossing that first time.

Suddenly Granny Fox lifted her head. "Hark!" she exclaimed.

Reddy pricked up his sharp, pointed ears. Way off back, in the direction from which they had come, they heard the baying of a dog. It wasn't the voice of Bowser the Hound but of a younger dog. Granny listened for a few minutes. The voice of the dog grew louder as it drew nearer.

"He certainly is following our track," said Granny Fox. "Now, Reddy, you run across the bridge and watch from the top of the little hill over there. Perhaps I can show you a trick that will teach you why I have made you learn to run across the bridge."

Reddy trotted across the long bridge and up to the top of the hill, as Granny had told him to. Then he sat down to watch. Granny trotted out in the middle of a field and sat down. Pretty soon a young hound broke out of the bushes, his nose in Granny's track. Then he looked up and saw her, and his voice grew still more savage and eager. Granny Fox started to run as soon as she was sure that the hound had seen her, but she did not run very fast. Reddy did not know what to make of it, for Granny seemed simply to be playing with the hound and not really trying to get away from him at all. Pretty soon Reddy heard another sound. It was a long, low rumble. Then there was a distant whistle. It was a train.

Granny heard it, too. As she ran, she began to work back toward the long bridge. The train was in sight now. Suddenly Granny Fox started across the bridge so fast that she looked like a little red streak. The dog was close at her heels when she started and he was so eager to catch her that he didn't see either the bridge or the train. But he couldn't begin to run as fast as Granny Fox. Oh, my, no! When she had reached the other side, he wasn't halfway across, and right behind him, whistling for him to get out of the way, was the train.

The hound gave one frightened yelp, and then he did the only thing he could do; he leaped down, down into the swift water below, and the last Reddy saw of him he was frantically trying to swim ashore.

"Now you know why I wanted you to learn to cross a bridge; it's a very nice way of getting rid of dogs," said Granny Fox, as she climbed up beside Reddy.

CHAPTER 3

BOWSER THE HOUND ISN'T FOOLED

REDDY FOX had been taught so much by Granny Fox that he began to feel very wise and very important. Reddy is naturally smart and he had been very quick to learn the tricks that old Granny Fox had taught him. But Reddy Fox is a boaster. Every day he swaggered about on the Green Meadows and bragged how smart he was. Blacky the Crow grew tired of Reddy's boasting.

"If you're so smart, what is the reason you always keep out of sight of Bowser the Hound?" asked

Blacky. "For my part, I don't believe that you are smart enough to fool him."

A lot of little meadow people heard Blacky say this, and Reddy knew it. He also knew that if he didn't prove Blacky in the wrong he would be laughed at forever after. Suddenly he remembered the trick that Granny Fox had played on the young hound at the railroad bridge. Why not play the same trick on Bowser and invite Blacky the Crow to see him do it? He would.

"If you will be over at the railroad bridge when the train comes this afternoon, I'll show you how easy it is to fool Bowser the Hound," said Reddy.

Blacky agreed to be there, and Reddy started off to find out where Bowser was. Blacky told everyone he met how Reddy Fox had promised to fool Bowser the Hound, and every time he told it he chuckled as if he thought it the best joke ever.

Blacky the Crow was on hand promptly that afternoon and with him came his cousin, Sammy Jay. Presently they saw Reddy Fox hurrying across the fields, and behind him in full cry came Bowser the Hound. Just as old Granny Fox had done with the young hound, Reddy allowed Bowser to get very near him and then, as the train came roaring along, he raced across the long bridge just ahead of it. He had thought that Bowser would be so intent on catching him that he would not notice the train until he was on the bridge and it was too late, as had been the case with the young hound. Then Bowser would have to jump down into the swift river or be run over.

As soon as Reddy was across the bridge, he jumped off the track and turned to see what would happen to Bowser the Hound. The train was halfway across the bridge, but Bowser was nowhere to be seen. He must have jumped already. Reddy sat down and grinned in the most self-satisfied way.

The long train roared past, and Reddy closed his eyes to shut out the dust and smoke. When he opened them again, he looked right into the wide-open mouth of Bowser the Hound, who was not ten feet away.

"Did you think you could fool me with that old trick?" roared Bowser.

Reddy didn't stop to make a reply; he just started off at the top of his speed, a badly frightened little fox.

You see, Bowser the Hound knew all about that trick and he had just waited until the train had passed and then had run across the bridge right behind it.

And as Reddy Fox, out of breath and tired, ran to seek the aid of Granny Fox in getting rid of Bowser the Hound, he heard a sound that made him grind his teeth.

"Haw, haw, haw! How smart we are!"

It was Blacky the Crow.

CHAPTER 4

REDDY FOX GROWS BOLD

REDDY FOX was growing bold. Everybody said so, and what everybody says must be so. Reddy Fox had always been very sly and not bold at all. The truth is Reddy Fox had so many times fooled Bowser the Hound and Farmer Brown's boy that he had begun to think himself very smart indeed. He had really fooled himself. Yes, Sir, Reddy Fox had fooled himself. He thought himself so smart that nobody could fool him.

Now it is one of the worst habits in the world to think too much of one's self. And Reddy Fox had the habit. Oh, my, yes! Reddy Fox certainly did have the habit! When anyone mentioned Bowser the Hound, Reddy would turn up his nose and say: "Pooh! It's the easiest thing in the world to fool *him.*"

You see, he had forgotten all about the time Bowser had fooled him at the railroad bridge. Whenever Reddy saw Farmer Brown's boy he would say with the greatest scorn: "Who's afraid of *him?* Not I!"

So as Reddy Fox thought more and more of his own smartness, he grew bolder and bolder. Almost every night he visited Farmer Brown's henyard. Farmer Brown set traps all around the yard, but Reddy always found them and kept out of them. It got so that Unc' Billy Possum and Jimmy Skunk didn't dare go to the henhouse for eggs any more, for fear that they would get into one of the traps set for Reddy Fox. Of course they missed those fresh eggs and of course they blamed Reddy Fox.

"Never mind," said Jimmy Skunk, scowling down on the Green Meadows where Reddy Fox was taking a sun bath, "Farmer Brown's boy will get him yet! I hope he does!" Jimmy said this a little spitefully and just as if he really meant it.

Now when people think that they are very, very smart, they like to show off. You know it isn't any fun at all to feel smart unless others can see how smart you are. So Reddy Fox, just to show off, grew very bold, very bold indeed. He actually went up to Farmer Brown's henyard in broad daylight, and almost under the nose of Bowser the Hound he caught the pet chicken of Farmer Brown's boy.

Ol' Mistah Buzzard, sailing overhead high up in the blue, blue sky, saw Reddy Fox and shook his bald head.

> *"Ah see Trouble on the way;*
> *Yes, Ah do! Yes, Ah do!*
> *Hope it ain't a-goin' to stay;*
> *Yes, Ah do! Yes, Ah do!*
> *Trouble am a spry ol' man,*
> *Bound to find yo' if he can;*
> *If he finds yo' bound to stick.*
> *When Ah sees him, Ah runs quick!*
> *Yes, Ah do! Yes, Ah do!"*

But Reddy Fox thought himself so smart that it seemed as if he really were hunting for Ol' Mr. Trouble. And when he caught the pet chicken of Farmer Brown's boy, Ol' Mr. Trouble was right at his heels.

CHAPTER 5

REDDY GROWS CARELESS

O L' MISTAH BUZZARD was right. Trouble was right at the heels of Reddy Fox, although Reddy wouldn't have believed it if he had been told. He had stolen that plump pet chicken of Farmer Brown's boy for no reason under the sun but to show off. He wanted everyone to know how bold he was. He thought himself so smart that he could do just exactly what he pleased and no one could stop him. He liked to strut around through the Green Forest and over the Green Meadows and brag about what he had done and what he could do.

Now people who brag and boast and who like to show off are almost sure to come to grief. And when they do, very few people are sorry for them. None of the little meadow and forest people liked Reddy Fox, anyway, and they were getting so tired of his boasting that they just ached to see him get into trouble. Yes, Sir, they just ached to see Reddy get into trouble.

Peter Rabbit, happy-go-lucky Peter Rabbit, shook his head gravely when he heard how Reddy had stolen that pet chicken of Farmer Brown's boy, and was boasting about it to everyone.

"Reddy Fox is getting so puffed up that pretty soon he won't be able to see his own feet," said Peter Rabbit.

"Well, what if he doesn't?" demanded Jimmy Skunk.

Peter looked at Jimmy in disgust.

> *"He comes to grief, however fleet,*
> *Who doesn't watch his flying feet.*

"Jimmy Skunk, if you didn't have that little bag of scent that everybody is afraid of, you would be a lot more careful where you step," replied Peter. "If Reddy doesn't watch out, someday he'll step right into a trap."

Jimmy Skunk chuckled. "I wish he would!" said he.

Now when Farmer Brown's boy heard about the boldness of Reddy Fox, he shut his mouth tight in a way that was unpleasant to see and reached for his gun. "I can't afford to raise chickens to feed foxes!" said he. Then he whistled for Bowser the Hound, and together they started out. It wasn't long before Bowser found Reddy's tracks.

"Bow, wow, wow, wow!" roared Bowser the Hound.

Reddy Fox, taking a nap on the edge of the Green Forest, heard Bowser's big, deep voice. He pricked up his ears, then he grinned. "I feel just like a good run today," said he, and trotted off along the Crooked Little Path down the hill.

Now this was a beautiful summer day and Reddy

knew that in summer men and boys seldom hunt foxes. "It's only Bowser the Hound," thought Reddy, "and when I've had a good run, I'll play a trick on him so that he will lose my track." So Reddy didn't use his eyes as he should have done. You see, he thought himself so smart that he had grown careless. Yes, Sir, Reddy Fox had grown careless. He kept looking back to see where Bowser the Hound was, but didn't look around to make sure that no other danger was near.

Ol' Mistah Buzzard, sailing round and round, way up in the blue, blue sky, could see everything going on down below. He could see Reddy Fox running along the edge of the Green Forest and every few minutes stopping to chuckle and listen to Bowser the Hound trying to pick out the trail Reddy had made so hard to follow by his twists and turns. And he saw something else, did Ol' Mistah Buzzard. It looked to him very much like the barrel of a gun sticking out from behind an old tree just ahead of Reddy.

"Ah reckon it's just like Ah said: Reddy Fox is goin' to meet trouble right smart soon," muttered Ol' Mistah Buzzard.

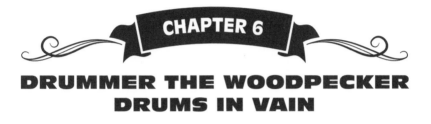

CHAPTER 6

DRUMMER THE WOODPECKER DRUMS IN VAIN

ONCE UPON A TIME, before he had grown to think himself so very, very smart, Reddy Fox would never, never have thought of running without watching out in every direction. He would have seen that thing that looked like the barrel of a gun sticking out from behind the old tree toward which he was running, and he would have been very suspicious, very suspicious indeed. But now all Reddy could think of was what a splendid chance he had to show all the little meadow and forest people what a bold, smart fellow he was.

So once more Reddy sat down and waited until Bowser the Hound was almost up to him. Just then Drummer the Woodpecker began to make a tremendous noise—rat-a-tat-tat-tat, rat-a-tat-tat-tat, rat-a-tat-tat-tat! Now everybody who heard that rat-a-tat-tat-tat knew that it was a danger signal. Drummer the Woodpecker never drums just that way for pleasure. But Reddy Fox paid no attention to it. He didn't notice it at all. You see, he was so full of the idea of his own smartness that he didn't have room for anything else.

"Stupid thing!" said Drummer the Woodpecker to himself. "I don't know what I am trying to warn him for, anyway. The Green Meadows and the Green Forest would be better off without him, a lot better off! Nobody likes him. He's a dreadful bully and is all the time trying to catch or scare to death those who are smaller than he. Still, he *is* so handsome!" Drummer cocked his head on one side and looked over at Reddy Fox.

Reddy was laughing to see how hard Bowser the Hound was working to untangle Reddy's mixed-up trail.

"Yes, Sir, he certainly is handsome," said Drummer once more.

Then he looked down at the foot of the old tree on which he was sitting, and what he saw caused Drummer to make up his mind. "I surely would miss seeing that beautiful red coat of his! I surely would!" he muttered. "If he doesn't hear and heed now, it won't be my fault!"

Then Drummer the Woodpecker began such a furious rat-a-tat-tat-tat on the trunk of the old tree that it rang through the Green Forest and out across the Green Meadows almost to the Purple Hills.

Down at the foot of the tree a freckled face on which there was a black scowl looked up. It was the face of Farmer Brown's boy.

"What ails that pesky woodpecker?" he muttered. "If he doesn't keep still, he'll scare that fox!"

He shook a fist at Drummer, but Drummer didn't appear to notice. He kept right on, rat-a-tat-tat-tat, rat-a-tat-tat-tat, rat-a-tat-tat-tat!

CHAPTER 7

TOO LATE
REDDY FOX HEARS

DRUMMER THE WOODPECKER was pounding out his danger signal so fast and so hard that his red head flew back and forth almost too fast to see. Rat-a-tat-tat-a-tat-tat, beat Drummer on the old tree trunk on the edge of the Green Forest. When he stopped for breath, he looked down into the scowling face of Farmer Brown's boy, who was hiding behind the old tree trunk.

Drummer didn't like the looks of that scowl, not a bit. And he didn't like the looks of the gun which Farmer Brown's boy had. He knew that Farmer

Brown's boy was hiding there to shoot Reddy Fox, but Drummer was beginning to be afraid that Farmer Brown's boy might guess what all that drumming meant—that it was a warning to Reddy Fox. And if Farmer Brown's boy did guess that, why—why—anyway, on the other side of the tree there was a better place to drum. So Drummer the Woodpecker crept around to the other side of the tree and in a minute was drumming harder than ever. Whenever he stopped for breath, he looked out over the Green Meadows to see if Reddy Fox had heard his warning.

But if Reddy had heard, he hadn't heeded. Just to show off before all the little meadow and forest people, Reddy had waited until Bowser the Hound had almost reached him. Then, with a saucy flirt of his tail, Reddy Fox started to show how fast he could run, and that is very fast indeed. It made Bowser the Hound seem very slow, as, with his nose to the ground, he came racing after Reddy, making a tremendous noise with his great voice.

Now Reddy Fox had grown as careless as he had grown bold. Instead of looking sharply ahead, he looked this way and that way to see who was watching and admiring him. So he took no note of where he was going and started straight for the old tree trunk on which Drummer the Woodpecker was pounding out his warning of danger.

Now Reddy Fox has sharp eyes and very quick ears. My, my, indeed he has! But just now Reddy was as deaf as if he had cotton stuffed in his ears. He was chuckling to himself to think how he was going to fool Bowser the Hound and how smart everyone would think him, when all of a sudden, he heard the rat-a-tat-tat-a-tat-tat of Drummer the Woodpecker and knew that that meant "Danger!"

For just a little wee second it seemed to Reddy Fox that his heart stopped beating. He couldn't stop running, for he had let Bowser the Hound get too close for that. Reddy's sharp eyes saw Drummer the Woodpecker near the top of the old tree trunk and noticed that Drummer seemed to be looking at something down below. Reddy Fox gave one quick look at the foot of the old tree trunk and saw a gun pointed at him and behind the gun the freckled face of Farmer Brown's boy. Reddy Fox gave a little gasp of fright and turned so suddenly that he almost fell flat. Then he began to run as never in his life had he run before. It seemed as though his flying feet hardly touched the grass. His eyes were popping out with fright as with every jump he tried to run just a wee bit faster.

Bang! Bang! Two flashes of fire and two puffs of smoke darted from behind the old tree trunk. Drummer the Woodpecker gave a frightened scream and flew deep into the Green Forest. Peter Rabbit flattened himself under a friendly bramble bush. Johnny Chuck dived headfirst down his doorway.

Reddy Fox gave a yelp, a shrill little yelp of pain, and suddenly began to go lame. But Farmer Brown's boy didn't know that. He thought he had missed and he growled to himself:

"I'll get that fox yet for stealing my pet chicken!"

CHAPTER 8

GRANNY FOX TAKES CARE OF REDDY

REDDY FOX was so sore and lame that he could hardly hobble. He had had the hardest kind of work to get far enough ahead of Bowser the Hound to mix his trail up so that Bowser couldn't follow it. Then he had limped home, big tears running down his nose, although he tried hard not to cry. "Oh! Oh! Oh!" moaned Reddy Fox, as he crept in at the doorway of his home.

"What's the matter now?" snapped old Granny Fox, who had just waked up from a sun nap.

"I—I've got hurt," said Reddy Fox, and began to cry harder.

Granny Fox looked at Reddy sharply. "What have you been doing now—tearing your clothes on a barbed-wire fence or trying to crawl through a bull-briar thicket? I should think you were big enough by this time to look out for yourself!" said Granny Fox crossly, as she came over to look at Reddy's hurts.

"Please don't scold, please don't, Granny Fox," begged Reddy, who was beginning to feel sick to his stomach as well as lame, and to smart dreadfully.

Granny Fox took one look at Reddy's wounds, and knew right away what had happened. She made Reddy stretch himself out at full length and then she went to work on him, washing his wounds with the greatest care and binding them up. She was very gentle, was old Granny Fox, as she touched the sore places, but all the time she was at work her tongue flew, and that wasn't gentle at all. Oh, my, no! There was nothing gentle about that!

You see, old Granny Fox is wise and very, very

sharp and shrewd. Just as soon as she saw Reddy's hurts, she knew that they were made by shot from a gun, and that meant that Reddy Fox had been careless or he never, never would have been where he was in danger of being shot.

"I hope this will teach you a lesson!" said Granny Fox. "What are your eyes and your ears and your nose for? To keep you out of just such trouble as this.

> *"A little Fox must use his eyes*
> *Or get someday a sad surprise.*
> *A little Fox must use his ears*
> *And know what makes each sound he hears.*
> *A little Fox must use his nose*
> *And try the wind where'er he goes.*
> *A little Fox must use all three*
> *To live to grow as old as me.*

"Now tell me all about it, Reddy Fox. This is summer and men don't hunt foxes now. I don't see how it happens that Farmer Brown's boy was waiting for you with a gun."

So Reddy Fox told Granny Fox all about how he had run too near the old tree trunk behind which Farmer Brown's boy had been hiding, but Reddy didn't tell how he had been trying to show off, or how in broad daylight he had stolen the pet chicken of Farmer Brown's boy. You may be sure he was very careful not to mention that.

And so old Granny Fox puckered up her brows and thought and thought, trying to find some good reason why Farmer Brown's boy should have been hunting in the summertime.

"Caw, caw, caw!" shouted Blacky the Crow.

The face of Granny Fox cleared. "Blacky the Crow has been stealing, and Farmer Brown's boy was out after him when Reddy came along," said Granny Fox, talking out loud to herself.

Reddy Fox grew very red in the face, but he never said a word.

CHAPTER 9

PETER RABBIT HEARS THE NEWS

JOHNNY CHUCK came running up to the edge of the Old Briarpatch quite out of breath. You see, he is so round and fat and roly-poly that to run makes him puff and blow. Johnny Chuck's eyes danced with excitement as he peered into the Old Briar-patch, trying to see Peter Rabbit.

"Peter! Peter Rabbit! Oh, Peter!" he called. No one answered. Johnny Chuck looked disappointed. It was the middle of the morning, and he had thought that Peter would surely be at home then. He would try once more.

"Oh, you Peter Rabbit!" he shouted in such a high-pitched voice that it was almost a squeal.

"What you want?" asked a sleepy voice from the middle of the Old Briar-patch.

Johnny Chuck's face lighted up. "Come out here, Peter, where I can look at you," cried Johnny.

"Go away, Johnny Chuck! I'm sleepy," said Peter Rabbit, and his voice sounded just a wee bit cross, for Peter had been out all night, a habit which Peter has.

"I've got some news for you, Peter," called Johnny Chuck eagerly.

"How do you know it's news to me?" asked Peter, and Johnny noticed that his voice wasn't quite so cross.

"I'm almost sure it is, for I've just heard it myself, and I've hurried right down here to tell you because I think you'll want to know it," replied Johnny Chuck.

"Pooh!" said Peter Rabbit, "it's probably as old as the hills to me. You folks who go to bed with the sun don't hear the news until it's old. What is it?"

"It's about Reddy Fox," began Johnny Chuck, but Peter Rabbit interrupted him.

"Shucks, Johnny Chuck! You *are* slow! Why, it was all over the Green Meadows last night how Reddy Fox had been shot by Farmer Brown's boy!" jeered Peter Rabbit. "That's no news. And here you've waked me up to tell me something I knew before you went to bed last night! Serves Reddy Fox right. Hope he'll be lame for a week," added Peter Rabbit.

"He can't walk at all!" cried Johnny Chuck in triumph, sure now that Peter Rabbit hadn't heard the news.

"What's that?" demanded Peter, and Johnny Chuck could hear him begin to hop along one of his little private paths in the heart of the Old Briar-patch. He knew now that Peter Rabbit's curiosity was aroused, and he smiled to himself.

In a few minutes Peter thrust a sleepy-looking face out from the Old Briar-patch and grinned rather sheepishly. "What was that you were saying about Reddy Fox?" he asked again.

"I've a good mind not to tell you, Mr. Know-it-all," exclaimed Johnny Chuck.

"Oh, please, Johnny Chuck," pleaded Peter Rabbit.

Finally Johnny gave in. "I said that Reddy Fox can't walk. Aren't you glad, Peter?"

"How do you know?" asked Peter, for Peter is very suspicious of Reddy Fox, and has to watch out for his tricks all the time.

"Jimmy Skunk told me. He was up by Reddy's house early this morning and saw Reddy try to walk. He tried and tried and couldn't. You won't have to watch out for Reddy Fox for some time, Peter. Serves him right, doesn't it?"

"Let's go up and see if it really is true!" said Peter suddenly.

"All right," said Johnny Chuck, and off they started.

CHAPTER 10

POOR REDDY FOX

PETER RABBIT and Johnny Chuck stole up the hill toward the home of Reddy Fox. As they drew near, they crept from one bunch of grass to another and from bush to bush, stopping behind each to look and listen. They were not taking any chances. Johnny Chuck was not much afraid of Reddy Fox, for he had whipped him once, but he was afraid of old Granny Fox. Peter Rabbit was afraid of both. The nearer he got to the home of Reddy Fox, the more anxious and nervous he grew.

POOR REDDY FOX

You see, Reddy Fox had played so many tricks to try and catch Peter that Peter was not quite sure that this was not another trick. So he kept a sharp watch in every direction, ready to run at the least sign of danger.

When they had tiptoed and crawled to a point where they could see the doorstep of the Fox home, Peter Rabbit and Johnny Chuck lay down in a clump of bushes and watched. Pretty soon they saw old Granny Fox come out. She sniffed the wind and then she started off at a quick run down the Lone Little Path. Johnny Chuck gave a sigh of relief, for he wasn't afraid of Reddy and now he felt safe. But Peter Rabbit was just as watchful as ever.

"I've got to see Reddy for myself before I'll go a step nearer," he whispered. Just then Johnny Chuck put a hand on his lips and pointed with the other hand. There was Reddy Fox crawling out of his doorway into the sun. Peter Rabbit leaned forward to see better. Was Reddy Fox really so badly hurt, or was he only pretending?

Reddy Fox crawled painfully out onto his doorstep. He tried to stand and walk, but he couldn't because he was too stiff and sore. So he just crawled. He didn't know that anyone was watching him, and with every movement he made a face. That was because it hurt so.

Peter Rabbit, watching from the clump of bushes, knew then that Reddy was not pretending. He knew that he had nothing, not the least little thing, to fear from Reddy Fox. So Peter gave a whoop of joy and sprang out into view.

Reddy looked up and tried to grin, but made a face of pain instead. You see, it hurt so to move.

"I suppose you're tickled to death to see me like this," he growled to Peter Rabbit.

Now Peter had every reason to be glad, for Reddy Fox had tried his best to catch Peter Rabbit to give to old Granny Fox for her dinner, and time and again Peter had just barely escaped. So at first Peter Rabbit had whooped with joy. But as he saw how very helpless Reddy really was and how much

pain he felt, suddenly Peter Rabbit's big, soft eyes filled with tears of pity.

He forgot all about the threats of Reddy Fox and how Reddy had tried to trick him. He forgot all about how mean Reddy had been.

"Poor Reddy Fox," said Peter Rabbit. "Poor Reddy Fox."

CHAPTER 11

GRANNY FOX RETURNS

U P OVER THE HILL trotted old Granny Fox. She was on her way home with a tender young chicken for Reddy Fox. Poor Reddy! Of course, it was his own fault, for he had been showing off and he had been careless or he never would have gone so near to the old tree trunk behind which Farmer Brown's boy was hiding.

But old Granny Fox didn't know this. She never makes such mistakes herself. Oh, my, no! So now, as she came up over the hill to a place where she could see her home, she laid the chicken down and then she crept behind a little bush and looked all over the Green Meadows to see if the way was clear. She knew that Bowser the Hound was chained up. She had seen Farmer Brown and Farmer Brown's boy hoeing in the cornfield, so she had nothing to fear from them.

Looking over to her doorstep, she saw Reddy Fox lying in the sun, and then she saw something else, something that made her eyes flash and her teeth come together with a snap. It was Peter Rabbit sitting up very straight, not ten feet from Reddy Fox.

"So that's that young scamp of a Peter Rabbit whom Reddy was going to catch for me when I was sick and couldn't! I'll just show Reddy Fox how easily it can be done, and he shall have tender young rabbit with his chicken!" said Granny Fox to herself.

So first she studied and studied every clump of grass and every bush behind which she could creep. She saw that she could get almost to where Peter Rabbit was sitting and never once show herself to him. Then she looked this way and looked that way to make sure that no one was watching her.

No one did she see on the Green Meadows who was looking her way. Then Granny Fox began to crawl from one clump of grass to another and from bush to bush. Sometimes she wriggled along flat on her stomach. Little by little she was drawing nearer and nearer to Peter Rabbit.

Now with all her smartness old Granny Fox had forgotten one thing. Yes, Sir, she had forgotten one thing. Never once had she thought to look up in the sky. And there was Ol' Mistah Buzzard sailing round and round and looking down and seeing all that was going on below.

Ol' Mistah Buzzard is sharp. He knew just what old Granny Fox was planning to do—knew it as well as if he had read her thoughts. His eyes twinkled.

"Ah cert'nly can't allow li'l' Brer Rabbit to be

hurt, Ah cert'nly can't!" muttered Ol' Mistah Buzzard, and chuckled.

Then he slanted his broad wings downward and without a sound slid down out of the sky till he was right behind Granny Fox.

"Do yo' always crawl home, Granny Fox?" asked Ol' Mistah Buzzard.

Granny Fox was so startled, for she hadn't heard a sound, that she jumped almost out of her skin. Of course Peter Rabbit saw her then, and was off like a shot.

Granny Fox showed all her teeth. "I wish you would mind your own business, Mistah Buzzard!" she snarled.

"Cert'nly, cert'nly, Ah sho'ly will!" replied Ol' Mistah Buzzard, and sailed up into the blue, blue sky.

CHAPTER 12

THE LOST CHICKEN

WHEN OLD GRANNY FOX had laid down the chicken she was bringing home to Reddy Fox to try to catch Peter Rabbit, she had meant to go right back and get it as soon as she had caught Peter. Now she saw Peter going across the Green Meadows, lipperty-lipperty-lip, as fast as he could go. She was so angry that she hopped up and down. She tore up the grass and ground her long, white teeth. She glared up at Ol' Mistah Buzzard, who had warned Peter Rabbit, but all she could do was to scold, and that didn't do her much good, for in a few minutes Ol' Mistah Buzzard was so far up in the blue, blue sky that he couldn't hear a word she was saying. My, my, but old Granny Fox certainly was angry! If she hadn't been so angry she might have seen Johnny Chuck lying as flat as he could make himself behind a big clump of grass.

Johnny Chuck was scared. Yes, indeed, Johnny Chuck was dreadfully scared. He had fought Reddy Fox and whipped him, but he knew that old Granny Fox would be too much for him. So it was with great relief that Johnny Chuck saw her stop tearing up the grass and trot over to see how Reddy Fox was getting along. Then Johnny Chuck crept along until he was far enough away to run. How he did run! He was so fat and roly-poly that he was all out of breath when he reached home, and so tired that he just dropped down on his doorstep and panted.

"Serves me right for having so much curiosity," said Johnny Chuck to himself.

Reddy Fox looked up as old Granny Fox came hurrying home. He was weak and very, very hungry. But he felt sure that old Granny Fox would bring him something nice for his breakfast, and as soon as he heard her footsteps his mouth began to water.

"Did you bring me something nice, Granny?" asked Reddy Fox.

Now old Granny Fox had been so put out by the scare she had had and by her failure to catch Peter Rabbit that she had forgotten all about the chicken she had left up on the hill. When Reddy spoke, she remembered it, and the thought of having to go way back after it didn't improve her temper a bit.

"No!" she snapped. "I haven't!—You don't deserve any breakfast anyway. If you had any gumption"—that's the word Granny Fox used, gumption—"if you had any gumption at all, you wouldn't have gotten in trouble, and could get your own breakfast."

Reddy Fox didn't know what gumption meant, but he did know that he was very, very hungry, and do what he would, he couldn't keep back a couple of big tears of disappointment. Granny Fox saw them.

"There, there, Reddy! Don't cry. I've got a fine fat chicken for you up on the hill, and I'll run back and get it," said Granny Fox.

So off she started up the hill to the place where she had left the chicken when she started to try to catch Peter Rabbit. When she got there, there wasn't any chicken. No, Sir, there was no chicken at all—just a few feathers. Granny Fox could hardly believe her own eyes. She looked this way and she looked that way, but there was no chicken, just a few feathers. Old Granny Fox flew into a greater rage than before.

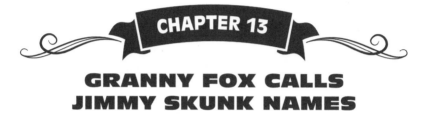

CHAPTER 13

GRANNY FOX CALLS JIMMY SKUNK NAMES

G RANNY FOX couldn't believe her own eyes. No, Sir, she couldn't believe her own eyes, and she rubbed them two or three times to make sure that she was seeing right. That chicken certainly had disappeared, and left no trace of where it had gone.

It was very queer. Old Granny Fox sat down to think who would dare steal anything from her. Then she walked in a big circle with her nose to the ground, sniffing and sniffing. What was she doing that for? Why, to see if she could find the tracks of anyone who might have stolen her chicken.

"Aha!" exclaimed old Granny Fox, starting to run along the top of the hill, her nose to the ground. "Aha! I'll catch him this time!"

In a few minutes she began to run more slowly, and every two or three steps she would look ahead. Suddenly her eyes snapped, and she began to creep almost flat on her stomach, just as she had crept for Peter Rabbit. But it wasn't Peter Rabbit this time. It was—who do you think? Jimmy Skunk! Yes, Sir, it was Jimmy Skunk. He was slowly ambling along, for Jimmy Skunk never hurries. Every big stick or stone that he could move, he would pull over or look under, for Jimmy Skunk was hunting for beetles.

Old Granny Fox watched him. "He must have a tremendous appetite to be hunting for beetles after eating my chicken!" muttered she. Then she jumped out in front of Jimmy Skunk, her eyes snapping, her teeth showing, and the hair on her back standing on end so as to make her look very

fierce. But all the time old Granny Fox took the greatest care not to get too near to Jimmy Skunk.

"Where's my chicken?" snarled old Granny Fox, and she looked very, very fierce.

Jimmy Skunk looked up as if very much surprised. "Hello, Granny Fox!" he exclaimed. "Have you lost a chicken?"

"You've stolen it! You're a thief, Jimmy Skunk!" snapped Granny Fox.

> *"Words can never make black white;*
> *Before you speak be sure you're right,"*

said Jimmy Skunk. "I'm not a thief."

"You are!" cried Granny working herself into a great rage.

"I'm not!"

"You are!"

All the time Jimmy Skunk was chuckling to himself, and the more he chuckled the angrier grew old Granny Fox. And all the time Jimmy Skunk kept moving toward old Granny Fox and Granny Fox kept backing away, for, like all the other little meadow and forest people, she has very great respect for Jimmy Skunk's little bag of scent.

Now, backing off that way, she couldn't see where she was going, and the first thing she knew she had backed into a bramble bush. It tore her skirts and scratched her legs. "Ooch!" cried old Granny Fox.

"Ha! ha! ha!" laughed Jimmy Skunk. "That's what you get for calling me names."

CHAPTER 14

GRANNY FOX FINDS WHAT BECAME OF THE CHICKEN

OLD GRANNY FOX was in a terrible temper. Dear, dear, it certainly was a dreadful temper! Jimmy Skunk laughed at her, and that made it worse. When he saw this, Jimmy Skunk just rolled over and over on the ground and shouted, he was so tickled. Of course, it wasn't the least bit nice of Jimmy Skunk, but you know that Granny Fox had been calling Jimmy a thief. Then Jimmy doesn't like Granny Fox anyway, nor do any of the other little meadow and forest people, for most of them are very much afraid of her.

When old Granny Fox finally got out of the bramble bush, she didn't stop to say anything more to Jimmy Skunk, but hurried away, muttering and grumbling and grinding her teeth. Old Granny Fox wasn't pleasant to meet just then, and when Bobby Coon saw her coming, he just thought it best to get out of her way, so he climbed a tree.

It wasn't that Bobby Coon was afraid of old Granny Fox. Bless you, no! Bobby Coon isn't a bit afraid of her. It was because he had a full stomach and was feeling too good-natured and lazy to quarrel.

"Good morning, Granny Fox. I hope you are feeling well this morning," said Bobby Coon, as old Granny Fox came trotting under the tree he was sitting in. Granny Fox looked up and glared at him with yellow eyes.

"It isn't a good morning and I'm not feeling fine!" she snapped.

"My goodness, how you have torn your skirts!" exclaimed Bobby Coon.

Old Granny Fox started to say something unpleasant. Then she changed her mind and instead she sat down and told Bobby Coon all her troubles. As she talked, Bobby Coon kept ducking his head behind a branch of the tree to hide a smile. Finally Granny Fox noticed it.

"What do you keep ducking your head for, Bobby Coon?" she asked suspiciously.

"I'm just looking to see if I can see any feathers from that chicken," replied Bobby Coon gravely, though his eyes were twinkling with mischief.

"Well, do you?" demanded old Granny Fox.

And just then Bobby Coon did. They were not on the ground, however, but floating in the air. Bobby Coon leaned out to see where they came from, and Granny Fox turned to look, too. What do you think they saw? Why, sitting on a tall, dead tree was Mr. Goshawk, just then swallowing the last of Granny's chicken.

"Thief! thief! robber! robber!" shrieked old Granny Fox.

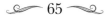

But Mr. Goshawk said nothing, just winked at Bobby Coon, puffed out his feathers, and settled himself for a comfortable nap.

CHAPTER 15

REDDY FOX HAS A VISITOR

H ARDLY WAS OLD GRANNY FOX out of sight on her way to hunt for the chicken she had left on the hill, when Unc' Billy Possum came strolling along the Lone Little Path. He was humming to himself, for he had just had a good breakfast. One of the Merry Little Breezes spied him and hurried to meet him and tell him about how Reddy Fox had been shot.

Unc' Billy listened, and the grin with which he had greeted the Merry Little Breeze grew into a broad smile.

"Are yo' all sure about that?" he asked.

The Merry Little Breeze was sure.

Unc' Billy Possum stopped for a few minutes and considered.

"Serves that no 'count Reddy Fox right," chuckled Unc' Billy. "He done spoil mah hunting at Farmer Brown's, he raised such a fuss among the hens up there. 'Tisn't safe to go there any mo'! No, Suh, 'tisn't safe, and it won't be safe for a right smart while. Did yo' say that Granny Fox is home?"

The Merry Little Breeze hadn't said anything about Granny Fox, but now remembered that she had gone up the hill.

"Ah believe Ah will just tote my sympathy over to Reddy Fox," said Unc' Billy Possum, as he started in the direction of Reddy Fox's house. But he made sure that old Granny Fox was not at home before he showed himself.

Reddy Fox lay on his doorstep. He was sick and sore and stiff. Indeed, he was so stiff he couldn't walk at all. And he was weak—weak and hungry,

dreadfully hungry. When he heard footsteps, he thought old Granny Fox was bringing him the chicken after which she had gone. He felt too ill even to turn his head.

"Did you get the chicken, Granny?" he asked weakly. No one answered. "I say, did you get the chicken, Granny?" Reddy's voice sounded a little sharp and cross as he asked this time.

Still there was no reply, and Reddy began to be a little bit suspicious. He turned over and raised his head to look. Instead of old Granny Fox, there was Unc' Billy Possum grinning at him.

> *"Smarty, Smarty is a thief!*
> *Smarty, Smarty came to grief!*
> *Tried to show off just for fun*
> *And ran too near a loaded gun.*

"Yo' alls cert'nly has got just what yo' deserve, and Ah'm glad of it! Ah'm glad of it, Suh!" said Unc' Billy Possum severely.

An angry light came into the eyes of Reddy Fox

and made them an ugly yellow for just a minute.
But he felt too sick to quarrel. Unc' Billy Possum
saw this. He saw how Reddy was really suffering,
and down deep in his heart Unc' Billy was truly
sorry for him. But he didn't let Reddy know it.
No, indeed! He just pretended to be tickled to
death to see Reddy Fox so helpless. He didn't dare
stay long, for fear Granny Fox would return. So,
after saying a few more things to make Reddy feel
uncomfortable, Unc' Billy started off up the Lone
Little Path towards the Green Forest.

"Too bad! Too bad!" he muttered to himself.
"If ol' Granny Fox isn't smart enough to get Reddy
enough to eat, Ah'll have to see what we-alls can
do. Ah cert'nly will."

CHAPTER 16

UNC' BILLY POSSUM
VISITS THE SMILING POOL

LITTLE JOE OTTER and Billy Mink were
sitting on the Big Rock in the Smiling Pool.
Because they had nothing else to do, they were
planning mischief. Jerry Muskrat was busy filling
his new house with food for the winter. He was too
busy to get into mischief.

Suddenly Billy Mink put a finger on his lips as
a warning to Little Joe Otter to keep perfectly still.
Billy's sharp eyes had seen something moving over
in the bulrushes. Together he and Little Joe Otter

watched, ready to dive into the Smiling Pool at the first sign of danger. In a few minutes the rushes parted and a sharp little old face peered out. Little Joe Otter and Billy Mink each sighed with relief, and their eyes began to dance.

"Hi, Unc' Billy Possum!" shouted Billy Mink.

A grin crept over the sharp little old face peering out from the bulrushes.

"Hi, yo'self!" he shouted, for it really was Unc' Billy Possum.

"What are you doing over here?" called Little Joe Otter.

"Just a-looking 'round," replied Unc' Billy Possum, his eyes twinkling.

"Have you heard about Reddy Fox?" shouted Billy Mink.

"Ah done jes' come from his home," replied Unc' Billy Possum.

"How is he?" asked Little Joe Otter.

"Po'ly, he sho'ly is po'ly," replied Unc' Billy Possum, shaking his head soberly. Then Unc' Billy

told Billy Mink and Little Joe Otter how Reddy Fox
was so stiff and sore and sick that he couldn't get
anything to eat for himself, and how old Granny
Fox had lost a chicken which she had caught for
him.

"Serves him right!" exclaimed Billy Mink, who
has never forgotten how Reddy Fox fooled him and
caught the most fish once upon a time.

Unc' Billy nodded his head. "Yo' are right.
Yo' cert'nly are right. Yes, Suh, Ah reckons yo'
are right. Was yo' ever hungry, Billy Mink—real
hungry?" asked Unc' Billy Possum.

Billy Mink thought of the time when he went
without his dinner because Mr. Night Heron had
gobbled it up, when Billy had left it in a temper. He
nodded his head.

"Ah was just a-wondering," continued Unc'
Billy Possum, "how it would seem to be right smart
powerful hungry and not be able to hunt fo'
anything to eat."

For a few minutes no one said a word. Then

Billy Mink stood up and stretched. "Good-by," said Billy Mink.

"Where are you going so suddenly?" demanded Little Joe Otter.

"I'm going to catch a fish and take it up to Reddy Fox, if you must know!" snapped Billy Mink.

"Good!" cried Little Joe Otter. "You needn't think that you can have all the fun to yourself either, Billy Mink. I'm going with you."

There was a splash in the Smiling Pool, and Unc' Billy Possum was left looking out on nothing but the Smiling Pool and the Big Rock. He smiled to himself as he turned away. "Ah reckon Ah'll sho' have to do my share, too," said he.

And so it happened that when old Granny Fox finally reached home with nothing but a little wood mouse for Reddy, she found him taking a nap, his stomach as full as it could be. And just a little way off were two fish tails and the feathers of a little duck.

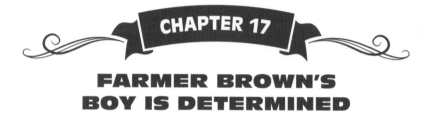

CHAPTER 17

FARMER BROWN'S BOY IS DETERMINED

FARMER BROWN'S boy had made up his mind. When he shut his teeth with a click and drew his lips together into a thin, straight line, those who knew him were sure that Farmer Brown's boy had made up his mind. That is just what he had done now. He was cleaning his gun, and as he worked he was thinking of his pet chicken and of all the other chickens that Reddy Fox had taken.

"I'm going to get that fox if it takes all summer!" exclaimed Farmer Brown's boy. "I ought to have gotten him the other day when I had a shot at him. Next time—well, we'll see, Mr. Fox, what will happen next time."

Now someone heard Farmer Brown's boy, heard everything he said, though Farmer Brown's boy didn't know it. It was Unc' Billy Possum, who was hiding in the very pile of wood on which Farmer Brown's boy was sitting. Unc' Billy pricked up his ears. He didn't like the tone of voice in which Farmer Brown's boy spoke. He thought of Reddy Fox still so stiff and sore and lame that he could hardly walk, all from the shot which Farmer Brown's boy thought had missed.

"There isn't goin' to be any next time. No, Suh, there isn't goin' to be any next time. Ah sho'ly doan love Reddy Fox, but Ah can't nohow let him be shot again. Ah cert'nly can't!" muttered Unc' Billy Possum to himself.

Of course, Farmer Brown's boy didn't hear him. He didn't hear him and he didn't see him when Unc' Billy Possum crept out of the back side of the

woodpile and scurried under the henhouse. He was too intent on his plan to catch Reddy Fox.

"I'm just going to hunt over the Green Meadows and through the Green Forest until I get that fox!" said Farmer Brown's boy, and as he said it he looked very fierce, as if he really meant it. "I'm not going to have my chickens stolen any more! No, Sir-e-e! That fox has got a home somewhere on the Green Meadows or in the Green Forest, and I'm going to find it. Then watch out, Mr. Fox!"

Farmer Brown's boy whistled for Bowser the Hound and started for the Green Forest.

Unc' Billy Possum poked his sharp little old face out from under the henhouse and watched them go. Usually Unc' Billy is grinning, but now there wasn't any grin, not the least sign of one. Instead Unc' Billy Possum looked worried.

"There goes that boy with a gun, and nobody knows what'll happen when it goes off. If he can't find Reddy Fox, just as likely as not he'll point it at somebody else just fo' fun. Ah hope he doan

meet up with mah Ol' Miz Possum or any of our li'l young'uns. Ah'm plumb afraid of a boy with a gun, Ah am. 'Pears like he doan have any sense. Ah reckon Ah better be moving along right smart and tell mah family to stay right close in the ol' hollow tree," muttered Unc' Billy Possum, slipping out from his hiding place. Then Unc' Billy began to run as fast as he could toward the Green Forest.

CHAPTER 18

THE HUNT FOR REDDY FOX

"Trouble, trouble, trouble, I feel it in the air;
Trouble, trouble, trouble, it's round me everywhere."

OLD GRANNY FOX muttered this over and over, as she kept walking around uneasily and sniffing the air.

"I don't see any trouble and I don't feel any trouble in the air. It's all in the sore places where I was shot," said Reddy Fox, who was stretched out on the doorstep of their home.

"That's because you haven't got any sense.

When you do get some and learn to look where you are going, you won't get shot from behind old tree trunks and you will be able to feel trouble when it is near, without waiting for it to show itself. Now I *feel* trouble. You go down into the house and stay there!" Granny Fox stopped to test the air with her nose, just as she had been testing it for the last ten minutes.

"I don't want to go in," whined Reddy Fox. "It's nice and warm out here, and I feel a lot better than when I am curled up way down there in the dark."

Old Granny Fox turned, and her eyes blazed as she looked at Reddy Fox. She didn't say a word. She didn't have to. Reddy just crawled into his house, muttering to himself. Granny stuck her head in at the door.

"Don't you come out until I come back," she ordered. Then she added: "Farmer Brown's boy is coming with his gun."

Reddy Fox shivered when he heard that. He didn't believe Granny Fox. He thought she was saying that just to scare him and make him stay inside. But he shivered just the same. You see he knew now what it meant to be shot, for he was still too stiff and sore to run, all because he had gone too near Farmer Brown's boy and his gun.

But old Granny Fox had not been fooling when she told Reddy Fox that Farmer Brown's boy was coming with a gun. It was true. He was coming down the Lone Little Path, and ahead of him was trotting Bowser the Hound. How did old Granny Fox know it? She just felt it! She didn't hear them, she didn't see them, and she didn't smell them; she just *felt* that they were coming. So as soon as she saw that Reddy Fox had obeyed her, she was off like a little red flash.

"It won't do to let them find our home," said Granny to herself, as she disappeared in the Green Forest.

First she hurried to a little point on the hill where she could look down the Lone Little Path. Just as she expected, she saw Farmer Brown's boy, and ahead of him, sniffing at every bush and all along the Lone Little Path, was Bowser the Hound. Old Granny Fox waited to see no more. She ran as fast as she could in a big circle which brought her out on the Lone Little Path below Farmer Brown's boy and Bowser the Hound, but where they couldn't see her, because of a turn in the Lone Little Path. She trotted down the Lone Little Path a very little way and then turned into the woods and hurried back up the hill, where she sat down and waited. In a few minutes she heard Bowser's great voice. He had smelled her track in the Lone Little Path and was following it. Old Granny Fox grinned. You see, she was planning to lead them far, far away from the home where Reddy Fox was hiding, for it would not do to have them find it.

And Farmer Brown's boy also grinned, as he heard the voice of Bowser the Hound.

"I'll hunt that fox until I get him," he said. You see, he didn't know anything about old Granny Fox; he thought Bowser was following Reddy Fox.

CHAPTER 19

UNC' BILLY POSSUM GIVES WARNING

"WHAT'S THE MATTER WITH YOU, Unc' Billy? You look as if you had lost your last friend." It was Jimmy Skunk who spoke.

Unc' Billy Possum stopped short. He had been hurrying so fast that he hadn't seen Jimmy Skunk at all.

"Matter enuff, Suh! Matter enuff!" said Unc' Billy Possum, when he could get his breath. "Do you hear that noise?"

"Sure, I hear that noise. That's only Bowser the

Hound chasing old Granny Fox. When she gets tired she'll lose him," replied Jimmy Skunk. "What are you worrying about Bowser the Hound for?"

"Bowser the Hound will have to be smarter than he is now befo' he can worry me, Ah reckon," said Unc' Billy Possum scornfully. "It isn't Bowser the Hound; it's Farmer Brown's boy and his gun!" Then Unc' Billy told Jimmy Skunk how he had been hiding in the woodpile at Farmer Brown's and had heard Farmer Brown's boy say that he was going to hunt over the Green Meadows and through the Green Forest until he got Reddy Fox.

"What of it?" asked Jimmy Skunk. "If he gets Reddy Fox, so much the better. Reddy always did make trouble for other people. I don't see what you're worrying about Reddy Fox for. He's big enough to take care of himself."

"Yo' cert'nly are plumb slow in your wits this morning, Jimmy Skunk, yo' cert'nly are plumb slow! Supposing yo' should meet up with Farmer Brown's boy with that gun in his hands and

supposing he had grown tired of watching fo'
Reddy Fox. That gun might go off, Jimmy Skunk;
it *might* go off when it was pointing right straight at
yo'!" said Unc' Billy Possum.

Jimmy Skunk looked serious. "That's so, Unc'
Billy, that's so!" he said. "Boys with guns do get
dreadfully careless, dreadfully careless. They don't
seem to think anything about the feelings of those
likely to get hurt when the gun goes off. What was
you thinking of doing, Unc' Billy?"

"Just passing the word along so everybody in
the Green Meadows and in the Green Forest will
keep out of the way of Farmer Brown's boy," replied
Unc' Billy Possum.

"Good idea, Unc' Billy! I'll help you," said
Jimmy Skunk.

So Unc' Billy Possum went one way, and Jimmy
Skunk went another way. And everyone they told
hurried to tell someone else. Happy Jack Squirrel
told Chatterer the Red Squirrel; Chatterer told
Striped Chipmunk, and Striped Chipmunk told

Danny Meadow Mouse. Danny Meadow Mouse told Johnny Chuck; Johnny Chuck told Peter Rabbit; Peter Rabbit told Jumper the Hare; Jumper the Hare told Prickly Porky; Prickly Porky told Bobby Coon; Bobby Coon told Billy Mink; Billy Mink told Little Joe Otter; Little Joe Otter told Jerry Muskrat, and Jerry Muskrat told Grandfather Frog. And everybody hastened to hide from Farmer Brown's boy and his terrible gun.

By and by Farmer Brown's boy noticed how still it was in the Green Forest. Nowhere did he see or hear a bird. Nowhere could he catch a glimpse of anybody who wore fur.

"That fox must have scared away all the other animals and driven away all the birds. I'll get him! See if I don't!" muttered Farmer Brown's boy, and never once guessed that they were hiding from him.

CHAPTER 20

OLD GRANNY FOX MAKES A MISTAKE

OLD GRANNY FOX was running through the overgrown old pasture, way up back of Farmer Brown's. She was cross and tired and hot, for it was a very warm day. Behind her came Bowser the Hound, his nose in Granny's tracks, and making a great noise with his big voice. Granny Fox was cross because she was tired. She hadn't done much running lately. She didn't mind running when the weather was cold, but now—"Oh dear, it is hot!" sighed old Granny Fox, as she stopped a minute to rest.

Now old Granny Fox is very, very smart and very, very wise. She knows all the tricks with which foxes fool those who try to catch them. She knew that she could fool Bowser the Hound and puzzle him so that he wouldn't be able to follow her track at all. But she wasn't ready to do that yet. No, indeed! Old Granny Fox was taking great care to see that her tracks were easy to follow. She wanted Bowser the Hound to follow them, although it made her tired and hot and cross. Why did she? Well, you see, she was trying to lead him, and with him Farmer Brown's boy, far, far away from the home where Reddy Fox was nursing the wounds that he had received when Farmer Brown's boy had shot at him a few days before.

"Bow, wow, wow!" roared Bowser the Hound, following every twist and turn which Granny Fox made, just as she wanted him to.

Back and forth across the old pasture and way up among the rocks on the edge of the mountain Granny Fox led Bowser the Hound. It was a long,

long, long way from the Green Meadows and the Green Forest. Granny Fox had made it a long way purposely. She was willing to be tired herself if she could also tire Bowser the Hound and Farmer Brown's boy. She wanted to tire them so that when she finally puzzled and fooled them and left them there, they would be too tired to go back to the Green Meadows.

By and by Granny Fox came to a hole in the ground, an old house that had once belonged to her grandfather. Now this old house had a back door hidden close beside the hollow trunk of a fallen tree. Old Granny Fox just ran through the house, out the back door, through the hollow tree, and then jumped into a little brook where there was hardly more than enough water to wet her feet. Walking in the water, she left no scent in her tracks.

Bowser the Hound came roaring up to the front door of the old house. Granny's tracks led right inside, and Bowser grew so excited that he made a tremendous noise. At last he had found where

Granny Fox lived; at least he thought he had. He was sure that she was inside, for there were her fresh tracks going inside and none coming out. Bowser the Hound never once thought of looking for a back door. If he had, he wouldn't have been any the wiser, because, you know, old Granny Fox had slipped away through the hollow tree trunk.

Granny Fox grinned as she listened to the terrible fuss Bowser was making. Then, when she had rested a little, she stole up on the hill where she could look down and see the entrance to the old deserted house. She watched Bowser digging and barking.

After a while a worried look crept into the face of old Granny Fox.

"Where's Farmer Brown's boy? I thought surely he would follow Bowser the Hound," she muttered.

CHAPTER 21

REDDY FOX DISOBEYS

WHEN OLD GRANNY FOX had sent Reddy Fox into the house and told him to stay there until she returned home, he had not wanted to mind, but he knew that Granny Fox meant just what she said, and so he had crawled slowly down the long hall to the bedroom, way underground.

Pretty soon Reddy Fox heard a voice. It was very faint, for you know Reddy was in his bedroom way underground, but he knew it. He pricked up his ears and listened. It was the voice of Bowser the

Hound, and Reddy knew by the sound that Bowser was chasing Granny Fox.

Reddy grinned. He wasn't at all worried about Granny Fox, not the least little bit. He knew how smart she was and that whenever she wanted to, she could get rid of Bowser the Hound. Then a sudden thought popped into Reddy's head, and he grew sober.

"Granny *did* feel trouble coming, just as she said," he thought.

Then Reddy Fox curled himself up and tried to sleep. He intended to mind and not put his little black nose outside until old Granny Fox returned. But somehow Reddy couldn't get to sleep. His bedroom was small, and he was so stiff and sore that he could not get comfortable. He twisted and turned and fidgeted. The more he fidgeted, the more uncomfortable he grew. He thought of the warm sunshine outside and how comfortable he would be, stretched out full length on the doorstep. It would take the soreness out of his legs.

Something must have happened to Granny to keep her so long. If she had known that she was going to be gone such a long time, she wouldn't have told him to stay until she came back, thought Reddy.

By and by Reddy Fox crept a little way up the long, dark hall. He could just see the sunlight on the doorstep. Pretty soon he went a little bit nearer. He wasn't going to disobey old Granny Fox. Oh, no! No, indeed! She had told him to stay in the house until she returned. She hadn't said that he couldn't *look* out! Reddy crawled a little nearer to the open door and the sunlight.

"Granny Fox is getting old and timid. Just as if my eyes aren't as sharp as hers! I'd like to see Farmer Brown's boy get near me when I am really on the watch," said Reddy Fox to himself. And then he crept a little nearer to the open door.

How bright and warm and pleasant it did look outside! Reddy just *knew* that he would feel ever and ever so much better if he could stretch out on the doorstep. He could hear Jenny Wren fussing

and scolding at someone or something, and he wondered what it could be. He crept just a wee bit nearer. He could hear Bowser's voice, but it was so faint that he had to prick up his sharp little ears and listen with all his might to hear it at all.

"Granny's led them way off on the mountain. Good old Granny!" thought Reddy Fox. Then he crawled right up to the very doorway. He could still hear Jenny Wren scolding and fussing. What does ail her?

> *If it's hot or if it's cold,*
> *Jenny Wren will always scold.*
> *From morn till night the whole day long*
> *Her limber tongue is going strong.*

"I'm going to find out what it means," said Reddy, talking to himself.

Reddy Fox poked his head out and—looked straight into the freckled face of Farmer Brown's boy and the muzzle of that dreadful gun!

CHAPTER 22

OL' MISTAH BUZZARD'S KEEN SIGHT

OLD GRANNY FOX had thought that when she fooled Bowser the Hound up in the old pasture on the edge of the mountain she could take her time going home. She was tired and hot, and she had planned to pick out the shadiest paths going back. She had thought that Farmer Brown's boy would soon join Bowser the Hound, when Bowser made such a fuss about having found the old house into which Granny Fox had run.

But Farmer Brown's boy had not yet appeared, and Granny Fox was getting worried. Could it be that he had not followed Bowser the Hound, after all? Granny Fox went out on a high point and looked, but she could see nothing of Farmer Brown's boy and his gun. Just then Ol' Mistah Buzzard came sailing down out of the blue, blue sky and settled himself on a tall, dead tree. Now Granny Fox hadn't forgotten how Ol' Mistah Buzzard had warned Peter Rabbit just as she was about to pounce on him, but she suddenly thought that Ol' Mistah Buzzard might be of use to her.

So old Granny Fox smoothed out her skirts and walked over to the foot of the tree where Ol' Mistah Buzzard sat.

"How do you do today, neighbor Buzzard?" inquired Granny Fox, smiling up at Ol' Mistah Buzzard.

"Ah'm so as to be up and about, thank yo'," replied Ol' Mistah Buzzard, spreading his wings out so that air could blow under them.

"My!" exclaimed old Granny Fox, "what splendid great wings you have, Mistah Buzzard! It must be

grand to be able to fly. I suppose you can see a great deal from way up there in the blue, blue sky, Mistah Buzzard."

Ol' Mistah Buzzard felt flattered. "Yes," said he, "Ah can see all that's going on on the Green Meadows and in the Green Forest."

"Oh, Mistah Buzzard, you don't really mean that!" exclaimed old Granny Fox, just as if she wanted to believe it, but couldn't.

"Yes, Ah can!" replied Ol' Mistah Buzzard.

"Really, Mistah Buzzard? Really? Oh, I can't believe that your eyes are so sharp as all that! Now I know where Bowser the Hound is and where Farmer Brown's boy is, but I don't believe you can see them," said Granny Fox.

Ol' Mistah Buzzard never said a word but spread his broad wings and in a few minutes he had sailed up, up, up until he looked like just a tiny speck to old Granny Fox. Now old Granny Fox had not told the truth when she said she knew where Farmer Brown's boy was. She thought she would trick Ol' Mistah Buzzard into telling her.

In a few minutes down came Ol' Mistah Buzzard. "Bowser the Hound is up in the old back pasture," said he.

"Right!" cried old Granny Fox, clapping her hands. "And where is Farmer Brown's boy?"

"Farmer Brown's boy is..." Ol' Mistah Buzzard paused.

"Where? Where?" asked Granny Fox, so eagerly that Ol' Mistah Buzzard looked at her sharply.

"Yo' said you knew, so what's the use of telling yo'?" said Ol' Mistah Buzzard. Then he added: "But if Ah was yo', Ah cert'nly would get home right smart soon."

"Why? Do, do tell me what you saw, Mistah Buzzard!" begged Granny Fox.

But Ol' Mistah Buzzard wouldn't say another word, so old Granny Fox started for home as fast as she could run.

"Oh dear, I do hope Reddy Fox minded me and stayed in the house," she muttered.

CHAPTER 23

GRANNY FOX HAS A TERRIBLE SCARE

OLD GRANNY FOX felt her heart sink way
down to her toes, for she felt sure Ol' Mistah
Buzzard had seen Farmer Brown's boy and his gun
over near the house where Reddy Fox was nursing
his wounds, or he wouldn't have advised her to
hurry home. She was already very tired and hot
from the long run to lead Bowser the Hound away
from the Green Meadows. She had thought to walk
home along shady paths and cool off, but now she
must run faster than ever, for she must know if

Farmer Brown's boy had found her house.

"It's lucky I told Reddy Fox to go inside and not come out till I returned; it's very lucky I did that," thought Granny Fox as she ran. Presently she heard voices singing. They seemed to be in the treetops over her head.

> *"Happily we dance and play*
> *All the livelong sunny day!*
> *Happily we run and race*
> *And win or lose with smiling face!"*

Granny Fox knew the voices, and she looked up. Just as she expected, she saw the Merry Little Breezes of Old Mother West Wind playing among the leaves. Just then one of them looked down and saw her.

"There's old Granny Fox! Just see how hot and tired she looks. Let's go down and cool her off!" shouted the Merry Little Breeze.

In a flash they were all down out of the treetops and dancing around old Granny Fox, cooling her off. Of course, Granny Fox kept right on running. She was too worried not to. But the Merry Little Breezes kept right beside her, and it was not nearly as hard running now as it had been.

"Have you seen Farmer Brown's boy?" panted Granny Fox.

"Oh, yes! We saw him just a little while ago over near your house, Granny Fox. We pulled his hat off, just to hear him scold," shouted the Merry Little Breezes, and then they tickled and laughed as if they had had a good time with Farmer Brown's boy.

But old Granny Fox didn't laugh—oh, my, no, indeed! Her heart went lower still, and she did her best to run faster. Pretty soon she came out on the top of the hill where she could look, and then it seemed as if her heart came right up in her mouth and stopped beating. Her eyes popped almost out of her head. There was Farmer Brown's boy standing right in front of the door of her home. And while she was watching, what should Reddy Fox do but stick his head out the door.

GRANNY HAS A SCARE

Old Granny Fox saw the gun of Farmer Brown's boy pointed right at Reddy and she clapped both hands over her eyes to shut out the dreadful sight. Then she waited for the bang of the gun. It didn't come. Then Granny peeped through her fingers. Farmer Brown's boy was still there, but Reddy Fox had disappeared inside the house.

Granny Fox sighed in relief. It had been a terrible scare, the worst she could remember.

CHAPTER 24

GRANNY AND REDDY HAVE TO MOVE

"I DON'T WANT TO MOVE," whined Reddy Fox. "I'm too sore to walk."

Old Granny Fox gave him a shove. "You go along and do as I say!" she snapped. "If you had minded me, we wouldn't have to move. It's all your own fault. The wonder is that you weren't killed when you poked your head out right in front of Farmer Brown's boy. Now that he knows where we live, he will give us no peace. Move along lively now! This is the best home I have ever had, and now I've got to leave it. Oh dear! Oh dear!"

Reddy Fox hobbled along up the long hall and out the front door. He was walking on three legs, and at every step he made a face because, you know, it hurt so to walk.

The little stars, looking down from the sky, saw Reddy Fox limp out the door of the house he had lived in so long, and right behind him came old Granny Fox. Granny sighed and wiped away a tear, as she said good-by to her old home. Reddy Fox was thinking too much of his own troubles to notice how badly Granny Fox was feeling. Every few steps he had to sit down and rest because it hurt him so to walk.

"I don't see the use of moving tonight, anyway. It would be a lot easier and pleasanter when the sun is shining. This night air makes me so stiff that I know I never will get over it," grumbled Reddy Fox.

Old Granny Fox listened to him for a while, and then she lost patience. Yes, Sir, Granny Fox lost patience. She boxed Reddy Fox first on one ear and then on the other. Reddy began to snivel.

"Stop that!" said Granny Fox sharply. "Do you want all the neighbors to know that we have got to move? They'll find it out soon enough. Now come along without any more fuss. If you don't, I'll just go off and leave you to shift for yourself. Then how will you get anything to eat?"

Reddy Fox wiped his eyes on his coat sleeve and hobbled along as best he could. Granny Fox would run a little way ahead to see that the way was safe and then come back for Reddy. Poor Reddy. He did his best not to complain, but it was *such* hard work. And somehow Reddy Fox didn't believe that it was at all necessary. He had been terribly frightened when he had disobeyed Granny Fox that afternoon and put his head out the door, only to look right into the freckled face of Farmer Brown's boy. He had ducked back out of sight again too quickly for Farmer Brown's boy to shoot, and now he couldn't see why old Granny Fox wanted to move that very night.

"She's getting old. She's getting old and timid and fussy," muttered Reddy Fox, as he hobbled along behind her.

It seemed to Reddy as if they had walked miles and miles. He really thought that they had been walking nearly all night when old Granny Fox stopped in front of the worst-looking old fox house Reddy had ever seen.

"Here we are!" said she.

"What! Are we going to live in that thing?" cried Reddy. "It isn't fit for any respectable fox to put his nose into."

"It is where I was born!" snapped old Granny Fox. "If you want to keep out of harm's way, don't go putting on airs now.

> *"Who scorns the simple things of life*
> *And tilts his nose at all he sees,*
> *Is almost sure to feel the knife*
> *Of want cut through his pleasant ease.*

"Now don't let me hear another word from you, but get inside at once!"

Reddy Fox didn't quite understand all Granny Fox said, but he knew when she was to be obeyed, and so he crawled gingerly through the broken-down doorway.

CHAPTER 25

PETER RABBIT MAKES A DISCOVERY

HARDLY HAD JOLLY, round, red Mr. Sun thrown off his nightcap and come out from his home behind the Purple Hills for his daily climb up in the blue, blue sky, when Farmer Brown's boy started down the Lone Little Path through the Green Forest.

Peter Rabbit, who had been out all night and was just then on his way home, saw him. Peter stopped and sat up to rub his eyes and look again. He wasn't quite sure that he had seen right the first time. But he had. There was Farmer Brown's boy,

sure enough, and at his heels trotted Bowser the
Hound.

Peter Rabbit rubbed his eyes once more and
wrinkled up his eyebrows. Farmer Brown's boy
certainly had a gun over one shoulder and a spade
over the other. Where could he be going down
the Lone Little Path with a spade? Farmer Brown's
garden certainly was not in that direction. Peter
watched him out of sight and then he hurried
down to the Green Meadows to tell Johnny Chuck
what he had seen. My, how Peter's long legs did fly!
He was so excited that he had forgotten how sleepy
he had felt a few minutes before.

Halfway down to Johnny Chuck's house, Peter
Rabbit almost ran plumb into Bobby Coon and
Jimmy Skunk, who had been quarreling and were
calling each other names. They stopped when they
saw Peter Rabbit.

"Peter Rabbit runs away
From his shadow, so they say.

Peter, Peter, what a sight!
Tell us why this sudden fright,"

shouted Bobby Coon.

Peter Rabbit stopped short. Indeed, he stopped
so short that he almost turned a somersault. "Say,"
he panted, "I've just seen Farmer Brown's boy."

"You don't say so!" said Jimmy Skunk,
pretending to be very much surprised. "You don't
say so! Why, now I think of it, I believe I've seen
Farmer Brown's boy a few times myself."

Peter Rabbit made a good-natured face at
Jimmy Skunk, and then he told all about how he
had seen Farmer Brown's boy with gun and spade
and Bowser the Hound going down the Lone Little
Path. "You know there isn't any garden down that
way," he concluded.

Bobby Coon's face wore a sober look. Yes, Sir, all
the fun was gone from Bobby Coon's face.

"What's the matter?" asked Jimmy Skunk.

"I was just thinking that Reddy Fox lives over in

that direction and he is so stiff that he cannot run," replied Bobby Coon.

Jimmy Skunk hitched up his trousers and started toward the Lone Little Path. "Come on!" said he. "Let's follow him and see what he is about."

Bobby Coon followed at once, but Peter Rabbit said he would hurry over and get Johnny Chuck and then join the others.

All this time Farmer Brown's boy had been hurrying down the Lone Little Path to the home old Granny Fox and Reddy Fox had moved out of the night before. Of course, he didn't know that they had moved. He put down his gun, and by the time Jimmy Skunk and Bobby Coon and Peter Rabbit and Johnny Chuck reached a place where they could peep out and see what was going on, he had dug a great hole.

"Oh!" cried Peter Rabbit, "he's digging into the house of Reddy Fox, and he'll catch poor Reddy!"

CHAPTER 26

FARMER BROWN'S BOY WORKS FOR NOTHING

THE GRASS AROUND the doorstep of the house where Reddy Fox had always lived was all wet with dew when Farmer Brown's boy laid his gun down, took off his coat, rolled up his shirt sleeves, and picked up his spade. It was cool and beautiful there on the edge of the Green Meadows. Jolly, round, red Mr. Sun had just begun his long climb up in the blue, blue sky. Mr. Redwing was singing for joy over in the bulrushes on the edge of the Smiling Pool. Yes, it was very beautiful, very beautiful indeed. It didn't seem as if harm could come to anyone on such a beautiful morning.

But there was Farmer Brown's boy. He had crawled on his hands and knees without making a sound to get near enough to the home of Reddy Fox to shoot if Reddy was outside. But there was no sign of Reddy, so Farmer Brown's boy had hopped up, and now he was whistling as he began to dig. His freckled face looked good-natured. It didn't seem as if he could mean harm to anyone. But there lay the gun, and he was working as if he meant to get to the very bottom of Reddy Fox's home!

Deeper and deeper grew the hole, and bigger and bigger grew the pile of sand which he threw out. He didn't know that anyone was watching him, except Bowser the Hound. He didn't see Johnny Chuck peeping from behind a tall bunch of meadow grass, or Peter Rabbit peeping from behind a tree on the edge of the Green Forest, or Bobby Coon looking from a safe hiding place in the top of that same tree. He didn't see Jimmy Skunk or Unc' Billy Possum or Happy Jack Squirrel or Digger the Badger. He didn't see one of them, but they saw him. They saw every shovelful of sand that he threw, and their hearts went pit-a-pat as they watched, for each one felt sure that something dreadful was going to happen to Reddy Fox.

Only Ol' Mistah Buzzard knew better. From way up high in the blue, blue sky he could look down and see many things. He could see all the little meadow and forest people who were watching Farmer Brown's boy. The harder Farmer Brown's boy worked, the more Ol' Mistah Buzzard chuckled to himself. What was he laughing at? Why, he could see the sharp face of old Granny Fox, peeping out from behind an old fence corner, and she was grinning. So Ol' Mistah Buzzard knew Reddy Fox was safe.

But the other little people of the Green Forest and the Green Meadows didn't know that old Granny Fox and Reddy Fox had moved, and their faces grew longer and longer as they watched Farmer Brown's boy go deeper and deeper into the ground.

"Reddy Fox has worried me almost to death and would eat me if he could catch me, but somehow things wouldn't be quite the same without him around. Oh dear, I don't want him killed," moaned Peter Rabbit.

"Perhaps he isn't home," said Jimmy Skunk.

"Of course he's home; he's so stiff and sore he can hardly walk at all and has to stay home," replied Johnny Chuck. "Hello, what's the matter now?"

Everybody looked. Farmer Brown's boy had climbed out of the hole. He looked tired and cross. He rested for a few minutes, and as he rested, he scowled. Then he began to shovel the sand back into the hole. He had reached the bottom and found no one there.

"Hurrah!" shouted Peter Rabbit and struck his heels together as he jumped up in the air.

And the others were just as glad as Peter Rabbit.

Johnny Chuck was especially glad, for, you see, Farmer Brown's boy had once found Johnny's snug home, and Johnny had had to move as suddenly as did Granny and Reddy Fox. Johnny knew just how Reddy must feel, for he had had many narrow escapes in his short life.

THE STORY OF

THORNTON W. BURGESS
BY CHRISTIE LOWRANCE

T
hornton Burgess was one of the most popular
and prolific American children's writers of the
20th century. His nature stories described in realistic
detail the lives of Reddy Fox, Jimmy Skunk, Peter
Cottontail, Chatterer the Red Squirrel and many
other wild creatures. The charming tales entertained
children, but they also explained how animals live
and how hard they have to work to survive.

Born on Cape Cod in 1874, young Thornton spent countless hours in nearby woods, fields, and shores. As he grew up, he realized he especially loved two things: nature and writing. He worked for many years as a journalist and photographer before authoring over 70 children's books, as well as writing 15,000 syndicated newspaper columns and nature newsletters for schools.

In the 1920s Burgess launched a children's nature program to bring science to an eager radio audience. Knowing that millions of children and adults listened to Burgess' opinions about nature, scientists and conservationists asked for his help in educating the public. Burgess used his popularity as a children's writer to support nature and wildlife causes, including migratory bird protection and anti-littering awareness.

Many natural science organizations honored Thornton Burgess for his influence on the environmental values of children around the world. At the end of his long literary career, Burgess believed his greatest achievement was that his life's work had taught children to respect nature and to be kind to wildlife.

HAVE YOU READ THESE OTHER ADVENTURES?

THE ADVENTURES OF PETER COTTONTAIL
128 Pages, $9.95 US/ £6.99 UK/ $12.95 CAN
ISBN: 9781633222922

The Adventures of Peter Cottontail recounts the hijinks of one of the most endearing and beloved creatures in children's literature. Full of mischief (and then remorse), Peter has exploits that are delightfully recognizable to anyone who has children and will surely tickle yet another generation of young readers.

**THE
THORNTON
BURGESS
LIBRARY**

THE ADVENTURES OF JIMMY SKUNK
128 Pages, $9.95 US/ £6.99 UK/ $12.95 CAN
ISBN: 9781633222939

Introduce a new generation to Thornton Burgess' Jimmy
Skunk. He may not be the biggest or the toughest fellow
in the Green Meadows, but he certainly has the respect of
everyone because of his special "perfume." Even so, there
are adventures to have and choices to make.

**THE
THORNTON
BURGESS
LIBRARY**

Brimming with creative inspiration, how-to projects, and useful information to enrich your everyday life, Quarto Knows is a favorite destination for those pursuing their interests and passions. Visit our site and dig deeper with our books into your area of interest: Quarto Creates, Quarto Cooks, Quarto Homes, Quarto Lives, Quarto Drives, Quarto Explores, Quarto Gifts, or Quarto Kids.

First Published in 2017 by Seagrass Press, an imprint of The Quarto Group. 6 Orchard Road, Suite 100, Lake Forest, CA 92630, USA.
T (949) 380-7510 **F** (949) 380-7575 **www.QuartoKnows.com**

Seagrass Press titles are also available at discount for retail, wholesale, promotional, and bulk purchase. For details, contact the Special Sales Manager by email at specialsales@quarto.com or by mail at The Quarto Group, Attn: Special Sales Manager, 401 Second Avenue North, Suite 310, Minneapolis, MN 55401 USA.

ISBN: 978-1-63322-368-4

Cover image: Maddie Frost
Interior illustrations: Harrison Cady
Author biography illustrations: Maddie Frost

Printed in China
10 9 8 7 6 5 4 3 2 1